OF PLUM PUDDINGS AND CARRIAGES

Of
PLUM PUDDINGS
and
CARRIAGES

JOY M CLAXTON

Matador
9 Priory Business Park,
Wistow Road, Kibworth Beauchamp,
Leicestershire. LE8 0RX
Tel: 0116 279 2299
Email: books@troubador.co.uk
Web: www.troubador.co.uk/matador
Twitter: @matadorbooks

ISBN 978 1789013 887

British Library Cataloguing in Publication Data.
A catalogue record for this book is available from the British Library.

Typeset in 14pt Aldine by Troubador Publishing Ltd, Leicester, UK

Matador is an imprint of Troubador Publishing Ltd

For Alison & in memory of Truett

FOREWORD

Joy Claxton, has given us a charming small book, *Of Plum Puddings and Carriages*. Here, the traditional carriage dogs, dalmatians, are placed into their home surroundings, the stables.

The adventures begin, from being puppies, to working adult dogs, their priorities to look after the Master's property, the carriage on its daily travels. Joy then describes and illustrates the wonderful variety of carriages within a stable yard, varying in body designs for the practical purpose of the carriage. Combined with the complex of skills required to maintain a carriage house, horses and harness.

This is a story of a dog's view, at ground level, explaining the multitude of spring attachments to the carriage body and axle.

This book is set to tell a fun story, but it also carries an educational theme, on the design and construction of the English carriage.

Colin Henderson
    Chairman of The Carriage Foundation.

PREFACE

Joy Claxton, is one of those special people who not only has a passion for horses but also in some small way has managed to make a modest living in the equine world. She has always been involved with horses, gaining much knowledge and enthusiasm from her time working with a well-known jobmaster.

Joy started her writing career some years ago, sharing her experiences in short stories and instructional manuals on the art of donkey driving.

Being an active member of the British Carriage Dog Society, Joy has always had a Dalmatian dog and her understanding of this special breed of carriage dog shines through in this charming short story about a litter of Dalmatian puppies. She transports the reader back in to a bygone era, with tales full of the dramas encountered in the time of horse-drawn carriages, bringing the past to life. Her line drawings and definitions of the vehicles are wonderfully accurate, enabling the reader to visualise the scenes she has described so vividly.

Caroline Dale-Leech MBE; L.H.H.I.
    Founder member of the Carriage Foundation.

INTRODUCTION

With this book the author hopes not only to entertain but to kindle an interest in carriages. An interest that she has had for many years, acquiring the knowledge she has through practical experience while working for various jobmasters and being among the 'old boys' whose reminiscences she loved to hear.

The younger groom and horse owner of this generation, who may be highly qualified by the BHS may be interested to know how problems were dealt with pre modern times. We now have lightweight rugs made from breathable modern textures and electrolyte and reviving drinks. Ready mixed feed is delivered in paper sacks and electricity powers our clippers.

By following the exploits of the Dalmatian puppies in their various homes, both town and country, she shows how some carriages were used and kept, though this is a book of fiction the information shown within certainly is not.

Types of Springs

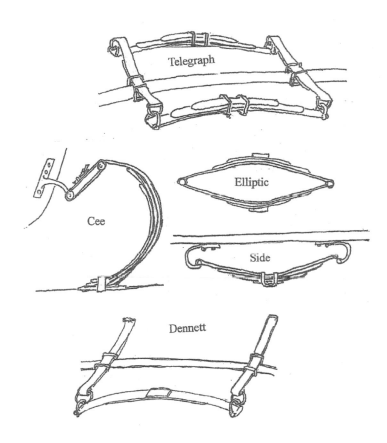

Telegraph

Cee

Elliptic

Side

Dennett

CHAPTER ONE

It had almost stopped raining now as Hilda ran across the cobbled yard, as she jumped the puddles the sack that she wore like a hood over her head flared out behind her. When she opened the little door set in the closed big double stable doors a warm smell of horse wafted forth and enveloped her. The smell she loved and had known all her short life, brought up in the manager's house of the small but busy jobmasters yard.

She went as quietly as her wooden clogs allowed down the passageway behind the stalls. The horses resting as they contentedly pulled the hay from their manger racks, their hindquarters catching the light from the one night lamp that gleamed from the shelf behind the far end standing.

Her father had said to her, as she ate her favourite supper of tripe and onions, 'Duchess is ready to receive visitors now'. So here she was leaning over the old door fixed across the end stall.

'Oh you clever girl' she murmured, Duchess lifted her head wagging her tail as she looked along her side at the four small white shapes snuggling into her as they sleepily fed. Hilda thought they looked like the little sweet plum puddings that her mother sometimes made that showed a few shadowy marks hinting at the fruits within.

Father had promised that she could choose their names, this was a responsible job, and she had been thinking about suitable names ever-since. Now the puppies were here at-last,she found there were three little dogs and just one bitch, she wondered what would their future be. She had already decided on her choice of names. She left the big stables as quietly as she had entered and hurried back indoors to her family. Announcing Lord, Duke, Earl and Queenie.

As the puppies grew, their coats acquired the spots and markings that they would have for the rest of their lives. Without being afraid of the horses they quickly learned to keep out of harm's way, steering clear from their stomping hooves. The carriage wheels held a fascination for them and they liked to accompany the various vehicles as they were wheeled out in to position on the yard and set ready for the horses to be put to them.

On a Sunday visit from her Grandparents, Grandpapa had taken an immediate interest in Duke and for some reason his name was changed to Quoss. Hilda was rather disappointed because she had put so much thought into choosing their names.

On either side of the big gateway from the street into the yard stood two long low buildings. The one to the left held the tackroom and the harness repair shop where Ernest, Hilda's elder brother worked. He was kept busy mending broken and worn harness that various traders brought to him. She loved to be with him, where it was cosy and warm and had the most lovely smell of leather. She would sit and watch as he cut and trimmed the hides, splicing and double stitching the straps. She had learned how to double stitch and had her own clam that she held firmly between her knees as they sat side by side. The tools of their trade set tidily in their places on the benchtop in front of them, the light streaming in from the long window above gave them good light to work by.

On this workbench there lay a collar with a soft lining, Boots the yard cat took up residence in it sleeping the mornings away after a night of hunting around the forage barns. She slept curled in it, a tight black furry ball occasionally stretching and putting out one of her white front paws, it was from these markings that she had got her name. A couple of times each year she became a mother, Hilda managed to find homes for the kittens amongst her school friends but sometimes she wondered where the tiny blind kittens had gone when the whole litter mysteriously vanished overnight. Their disappearance she noticed happened when her brother went to the riverside pub carrying a small sack.

Hilda still went to school most mornings even though she was nearly nine, she could read as well as write and add up and take away. Boring things that her mother said would stand her in good stead though she would much rather be doing useful things about the yard. Jobs that she was getting quite proficient with and she knew that she was real help to Ernest. Concentrating as she pushed her two needles in opposite directions. One after the other through the same hole she had made with her awal and then pulling the waxed thread tight to make a strong stitch.

She also loved to groom and harness the horses, they held their heads down so that she could gently brush their faces or so that she could push the heavy collar and hames over their heads even though she was too short to reach. The kindly animals lowered their heads then she could turn the collar behind their ears, always in the direction that their mane grew. Her Father had made her a box that she stood on to reach the places she couldn't from the floor. How she wished she was a boy and could wear trousers not a dress and pinafore that had silly frills down the straps. While the horses were out working she loved to brush out their hay racks and sponge clean the mangers and water bowls, before putting more sweet smelling hay in the rack and fresh water into the bowl. Each stall had its own heavy manger block fixed right across the front wall, the ones used in her Father's yard were a little unusual in that they had a built-in water bowl, father had insisted on these as when he awoke in the night he would like to take a sip of water from his glass that stood next to his side of the bed. Why should a horse be any different in feeling thirsty in the night? In this manger block there was a hole, through this a rope ran, one end buckled on to the horses head collar, at the other end was tied a heavy wooden log, this kept the tierope running smoothly allowing the horse the freedom to move his head but preventing it from getting a leg entangled over it while still keeping the horse secured.

The building on the other side of the yard's entrance was the Forge, here the shoes for the horses were made and the farrier worked. Having prized the old worn shoes off he then clipped and trimmed the feet, rasping away at the horn to make a fresh, clean and level surface to fit the new shoes on to.

The puppies watched, each one waiting in turn for the trimmings to be thrown down to them, then taking its prize to gnaw and eat in peace under a nearby vehicle before going back for another tasty morsel. The yard was filled with the sounds of ringing, made by the double clang from the hammer as the shoes were shaped on the anvil from the metal rods brought glowing red hot from the blacksmith's fire. Then a cloud of blue acrid smoke would appear as the farrier held the hot shoe against the horses insensitive hoof, the burned stain making a pattern showing him how the shoes needed to be altered to make a comfortable fit. The shoes were plunged into a bucket of water to cool, this produced lots of bubbling and steam. Then the shoes were ready and finally nailed in place.

The puppies were growing fast and now that Duchess's milk had dried up Hilda fed them on scraps from the family's kitchen. The butcher's lad who drove his family's beautifully painted delivery cart, brought lights and offal from their shop, along with the gristly trimmings from the cuts of meat that their discerning customers had ordered. Often the tradesmen who brought their horses to be shod ate their lunchtime bait while waiting for the farrier to finish his work. They would throw down their leftover crusts and pastries, the pups scrabbled for these and devoured them, much to the dismay of the hens that strutted and scraped in the yard as they foraged for food around the muckheap. One of Hilda's job's each day was to search the hay and straw barns for their eggs.

She had tried not to get too fond of the little dogs as she knew that they would soon have to be going away to their new homes. She watched them now as they played some boisterous noisy game of tug-of-war. To her horror she saw what they were tugging and destroying it was one of the button-through seat cushions from the canoe-shaped Landau, they had been put out to air in the sunshine while the Landau itself was being washed.

Rushing forward shouting, 'no, no leave it you bad dogs' she retrieved the cushion, its horse hair pad was pulled out of shape and its covering of dark blue Melton cloth ripped beyond repair.

The puppies skulked away and gathered under the butcher's cart, this was one of their favourite places to be as to them, with their sensitive noses, it still smelled deliciously of meat that had been in its cupboard-like locker even though it was scrubbed out each day when the cart was washed. This cart was well-kept, its paintwork pristine as while out on the delivery round it advertised the quality of the meat that could be procured from the family butchers, whose name was inscribed on the side. It had an accurately detailed painting of a bull's head on the door of the locker that had little louvred vents set in to the front of it, so that as the smart pony trotted along cool air passed over the meat inside. This had been parcelled up in brown paper and tied with string ready for the order to be delivered to the kitchen doors.

Hilda having scolded the pups retrieved the cushion and showed it to her father who was very cross! Instead she found a frayed piece of rope so that they could continue their pretend growling and pulling game. Earl who found himself temporarily excluded spied Boots wandering across the yard making her way from her night's hunting in the feed shed towards the harness shop. Immediately he took chase but she ran to the safety of the Hansom Cab that had just returned from a long night's hire with its tired horse being led to his stable. With Earl and Queenie hot on her tail she leapt up on to the apron floor of the cab and turned, hissing and snarling before jumping higher to balance on the narrow curved dashboard. Naughty Earl had received a painful smack on his nose from needle-like claws, yelping he ran away, his fun spoiled. Boots quickly gained the sanctuary of her collar bed for her mornings sleep.

From many scoldings the puppies had learned not to chase the chickens and were now peacefully sharing the shade with them one scorching hot day. The sun beating down onto the cobbles of the yard had made them so hot, it was quite uncomfortable for their feet. They had sought relief of the shade under the big Charabanc that had been prepared for the Sunday school excursion the next day, when the members of the local Methodist Chapel were to go out into the countryside for a picnic and games. The four large wheels carried a canoe-shaped body with seating for 20 or so. The passengers had to climb up a set of five steps that curved up the back of the vehicle to sit facing forward on the slatted seats, and were sheltered from the sun by a jolly red and white striped awning. On either side of the stairs little slatted doors opened in to the body of the carriage providing storage for food and drink.

As much as Hilda loved the puppies she was finding their antics rather wearing, she was continually picking up grooming brushes that had been scattered over the yard and returning them to the their box that was set on a shelf in the big stable, but Lord had acquired the knack of jumping up and knocking it down so that he could run off with a brush and play with it.

Her father was thatching a tired wet horse that stood gently steaming in its stall when she was returning yet another dandy brush. He spoke to her as he rolled two big handfuls of straw into long sausage shapes, then pushed them under the rug along the horses back to let the steam out, while keeping the horse warm.

'You know that it's time for the pups to go now, they should've gone some weeks ago'. Words that she had dreaded to hear. 'I have decided that we will keep Queenie but the others must go this week'.

She was so glad that Queenie was to stay as the little bitch and she had grown fond of each other, accompanying her on her morning egg hunts and then sitting beside her while she stitched, mending bits of harness. She was always with her while Hilda attended to the mangers and set the stables fair enjoying the task of making the stalls clean and comfy for the returning tired horses. 'Quess is to go to Grandpapa at the wharf, you take can take him on the omnibus tomorrow.'

Chapter Two

The next day, having eaten her bread and dripping lunch, Hilda put a halter rope round Quess's neck and they set off together. Though he hadn't really been on a lead before he was very good and didn't pull as they walked to where the Omnibus would stop. While they waited they watched the various cabs, carts and carriages that crowded the road. Most of them were carts and dreys drawn by shires and heavy types of horses, but there were a few smart delivery vans. Their drivers dressed in a formal style and driving some very nice animals.

When the Omnibus drew up she asked its conductor if they could please come aboard and paid him the coin that her mother had given her. They scrambled up the little curved stairway to the roof and made their way to the front where they sat on the garden-seat like bench. Looking down over the driver's shoulder onto the broad back of the pair he drove, the reins coming up steeply to his hands from the terrets of the hames. They enjoyed their drive and seeing the River Thames, brown and rapidly surging beneath them while they crossed Waterloo Bridge, then it was time for them to get off. They found it far more difficult going down the stairs than it had been to go up them. Then they made the short walk to the wharf where her grandparents lived.

Hilda and Quess followed a horse and cart into the vestry yard and watched as it made its way along the wharf. It stopped and turned, the horse cleverly crossing its legs as he backed the huge cart up to the chute, where the refuse, filth and grime picked up off the city streets was shovelled out, falling down into the waiting barge floating below. She saw other horses taken out of their shafts go to the water trough and having drunk their fill they made their own way up the ramp leading to the upstairs stables

for their feed and night's rest, their stalls littered down with peat, making a soft bed for their tired legs and feet.

She saw her uncle, foreman of the wharf, talking to some of the drivers. As he turned he noticed the pair. 'Ah there you are, your grandmother is expecting you, you will find her in the kitchen.' As he indicated the door it opened wide and grandmama appeared smiling a welcome as she wiped her hands on her apron, 'Come on in tea is ready'.

Hilda soon found herself sitting at the table with an array of ham and pickles accompanied by crusty bread spread with plenty of butter and little Welsh cakes warm off the griddle. Quess scoffed off a bowl of meat and gravy set before him then settled down making himself at home on the mat beside the range. The pup was lucky because he was not only to be a yard dog but a house dog as well and to be a companion to Grandpapa in his old age.

When tea was finished and she had helped clear and wash the dishes she settled herself down on Grandpapa's lap as he sat in his comfy chair beside the range. 'Why did you change Duke's name?' she asked, he made sucking sounds as he drew on his pipe. 'Well it's like this' he began 'When I was about your age I lived with my ma and pa above the stables of a big country house. I worked as a stable boy but my father was the head coachman to this titled family. When the grandson was married he planned to take his bride for a three-month honeymoon onto the continent, rather like a little Grand Tour.'

'What is a Grand Tour?' Hilda interrupted.

'That was a journey a lot of wealthy young men made. They travelled in their own comfy carriages all over the continent, Italy, Switzerland and Germany were very popular. Visiting many of the interesting places they got grand ideas of remodelling their mansions and filling them with lovely sculptures, furniture and paintings that they bought and sent home to beautify them'. Grandpapa stopped and thought, closing his eyes as he remembered, after a moment he went on. 'They travelled very often with the same horses, sometimes as much as fifty miles a day, stopping to rest and feed the horses about every ten miles or so, while the master and his companion visited some place of interest. They had the help of a mounted courier who rode ahead, planning the route and stops for them as they travelled'.

He went on to tell her that the old carriage that the grandpa and his cousin the Marquis had used for their Grand Tour, was still in the coach house, it was pulled out and looked at with a view to refurbishing it for the honeymoon, but the Marquis decided that they would be more comfortable if they had a modern carriage, and it would be of more use to them in their future life together. As he was not only uncle but godfather to the young man he commissioned and paid for a Britzka to be built for them. This carriage was long enough for them to lie down in and be cosy behind a

folding panel of little glass windows that fitted into the hood, or to be an open carriage when they preferred.

Off they all went on their continental journey and just like in times past a Dalmatian appeared from nowhere and attached himself to them, running with the horses all day and sleeping under the Brizka at night.

Hilda thought the story had ended and her grandpapa had gone to sleep but he hadn't, he was just collecting his thoughts and then continued. 'It was one of those dreadful wet days with rain and sleet coming down at them like arrows, they were glad when they arrived at the Inn, where they were to spend the night. They hurried inside into the warm taking only what was needed for the night's stay.' 'My father', he said 'was glad to get his horses in the warm stables and attend to them, and the Britzka was hurriedly pushed under an open-fronted barn beside several more carriages that had brought other guests'.

'In the middle of the night with the rain still beating on the windows the young bride suddenly woke, remembering that she had left her jewels in the carriage, tearfully she informed her husband of her mistake. They both worried and as soon as it was light they went downstairs, only to be told that robbers had come in the night intent on stealing any valuables left in the carriages'. Unseen by the robbers, the dog, well camouflaged by his dark spots had frightened them off and all was well. The grateful couple kept the dog, bringing him home with them and called him Quess after their benefactor.' Grandpapa bent down and gently stroked the sleeping puppy.

While Hilda had been listening her grandmama had been rummaging through the drawers of the dresser that stood in the warm living room, having found what she was looking for she came with an old sketchbook in her hand and showed her a portrait. It was drawn in pen and ink and was of a Dalmatian, underneath it was written 'Marquis'. Hilda looked at it and then at the sleeping puppy comparing their markings, they were very much alike, in fact almost the same. 'Who drew this?' she said. 'Your great grandpapa, he was quite a good artist and he wrote some rhyming verse too. Would you like me to read one to you?' As Hilda sat snugly on her grandfather's lap in her imagination she was transported into the past as grandmama read to her.

The travellers are ready, to return home again
they must travel the byways, the road and the lane.
The horses harnessed and put to for the day
were a nice sort of chestnut and a black-pointed bay.
With wheels all arumble the coach dips and sways
as it merrily speeds along the highways.

On soft cushions the travellers take their ease
as they are driven through light-dappled tunnels of trees.
From brocaded comfort they view hill and dale
in the knowledge that they are guarded well.

Their spotted guardians run and leap
while easily to the horses speed they keep.
Sometimes close to the wheels they trot and run
Or under the axle shaded from the sun.
On wide verges that the swaying carriage passes
there are a myriad of flowers among the grasses,
oxeyed daisies, flax and scabius grow
nodding their heads as the breezes blow.
Upwards the road steadily climbs
'cross downland and heath it meanders and winds.

Dark gorse bushes crowd close to the road
just where the long hill makes the horses lean in to their load
and slacken speed. Robbers await in hiding,
As the carriage draws close they hear the coachman chiding
his pair, out steps the man a bridle he's caught
pulling the plunging horses as in fear they fought
to keep their feet on the backward slope.
The other man comes out and shouts in hope
as the carriage with a lurch and rock
slews to one side and comes to a stop.
He demands, 'throw down your jewels and purses',

but the traveller denies him with many curses
as he knows that his guardians are near,
that the robbers will retreat in confusion and fear.
As a team the dogs who work together
are silently crossing the heathland heather.
The bitch with one huge silent bound
knocks that robber to the ground.
Scrambling up quickly makes his exit
as away over the heath he legs it.

The dog holds the first man with such a growling stare
he quickly releases the head of the frightened mare.
As painfully through the gorse bushes he ran
cursing Dalmatians who played no part in his plan.
And the dogs? Retreating robbers is what they see
as they bark and wag their tails triumphantly
and with one last loud bark,
think it a game, quite a lark.

They quickly catch up with their coach again
as it drives away along the lane,
faithfully trotting each on its station,
our loyal friends the Dalmatian.

Hilda slept and never noticed that her father had come to fetch her home. By arrangement he had been driving two ladies who had booked him for an afternoon's London shopping trip. Having taken them and their purchases back to their home in fashionable Dulwich, he had made a short detour and was now here to take her home again. He lifted her, cuddling her gently against his shoulder and carefully laid her on the cushioned bench seat in the Brougham where she slept until they were home.

CHAPTER THREE

Next morning Hilda had another journey to make, this time with Lord who was not nearly as well behaved on the lead as his brother had been. He was very strong, it seemed as though he was anxious to get to wherever it was that they were going. It was hard work as they pulled each other along the pavements, and it was really quite frightening crossing roads that were busy with all sorts of vehicles, every one of them hurrying as they went about their business.

The route that Hilda had chosen to take that hot autumn morning took them beside the Park. Through the trees she could see gentlemen and ladies riding at a sedate pace along Rotten Row. Walking spectators showed off their latest fashions while they watched the many smart carriages parading along the carriage drive, the wealthy occupants taking the air enjoying this popular pastime of socialising with each other.

At Hyde Park corner Hilda had to haul Lord to a stop at the curbside as a beautiful Landau approached and swept past through the entrance and onto the Park Drive. It

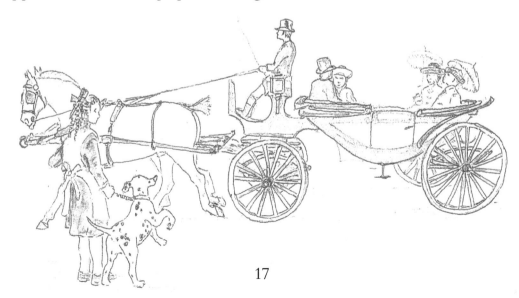

was none other than their own carriage, her father as coachman sat tall and straight, looking so smart in his silk top hat and dark livery coat as he drove his matched pair of liver chestnuts who stepped in stride with one another. The elderly lady who had hired them for the morning sat comfortably enjoying the warm sunshine, as both the folding heads were laid right back making it an open carriage. She was chaperoning her two nieces, one shaded her face with her parasol while talking with the handsome young man sitting opposite. Hilda giggled to herself on seeing the ladies wide-brimmed hats almost collided as they conversed, she waved to her father but as he was on duty he only acknowledged her with a wink as he continued on. They were followed by another Landau, though just as nicely turned out, it lacked the elegance of the sweeping lines of her father's canoe-shaped carriage as it was a well-bottomed Landau with its rather square shape, it seemed to her to be rather clumpy.

Lord and Hilda continued on their way finding it hot, dusty and smelly in the narrow streets away from the Park and managing the big strong puppy took all of her strength. She was glad when they safely arrived in Berkeley Square and could pause to

rest and sit on the grass under the great plane trees that grew there. She admired the imposing grey stone mansions that faced on to the square with their big, shiny black front doors set above a few wide steps, while either side speared top railings edged the pavements protecting the drop to the cellars.

Her uncle was coachman to a family who resided in one of these mansions. He and Auntie with her cousins, lived above the coach-house and stables in the Mews behind. Lord tugged Hilda along Charles Street that led from the square, then with a plunging surge off into the Mews, it was just as if he knew that this was where they were going.

Outside the coach-house the cobbles were wet where her uncle had just washed off the Brougham that had been used earlier that morning, he was now drying and polishing it off with a large chamois leather. He smiled a welcome at the two of them

and called out, 'Jake, your puppy is here.' Immediately her ginger-haired cousin appeared, squatting down he made a huge fuss of Lord who bounded about, licking his face and ears and finally pushed him over into a puddle, but Jake didn't seem to mind one bit. Picking himself up he helped his father push the Brougham back into the coach house before taking Lord's leads from Hilda. She followed them into the dim coach house where she could see two more carriages.

A Ladies Phaeton and, like a George the Fourth Phaeton it had a huge elegantly curved splash, this the young ladies of the house drove in the Park each day and Lord, when he was full-grown, would accompany. Further along stood the families' Town Coach. The dark shiny body of the coach hanging on its broad leather straps lying over the curved Cee springs above the maroon-coloured wheels. The sumptuous Hammer Cloth over

the coachman's seat glowed with gold braid and tassles. Hilda only got a fleeting glimpse of these vehicles as she was hustled along, past tall glass-fronted cupboards in which she could see the sets of harness used with them, hanging ready for use.

She found herself in a wide passage-like room set under the slope of the stairs. She wasn't quite sure of the purpose of this room as it had bags of chaff and feed bins in it, also a harness cleaning hook and table with a single set of harness strewn upon it, that obviously Jake had been in the process of cleaning when she had arrived. On the wood-panelled walls there were racks with bridles and saddles hanging on them. A pot-bellied stove that, though it was not alight today, would keep things warm and dry in the winter months. In one corner near this, a light chain was fixed to the wall beside a raised platform on which some old rugs had been placed, this was to be Lord's bed, comfortably above any drafts on the floor. He hardly noticed as Jake clipped the chain to his collar because there was a meaty shin-bone provided for his welcome.

Hilda was ushered into the adjoining stable where four horses stood in the curved top standings. A pair of big Cleveland Bays suitable for the Town Coach that was now only occasionally used, though they took their turn as a single, put to the Brougham every day when the master of the house was driven to his place of business in the city. Next to them were an elegant dun-coloured pair that the daughters either drove or rode side saddle in the Park along Rotten Row.

Jake opened what Hilda thought was a cupboard door, only to reveal a steep, narrow staircase that led upstairs to a little kitchen in a corner of the living room. It was very hot in here on this early autumn morning, on the black range a kettle on the grate sang, ready for the pot of tea that Aunty was about to make. She came bustling through from the adjoining bedroom saying that she expected Hilda would like a brew before going home. They sat chatting for a while and ate some freshly-made dropscones off her griddle. It had been quite a long walk from home and now having drunk several cups of tea Hilda wondered where the toilet was. She could see a door the other side of the stairs but it only accessed the hayloft where Jake had his truckle bed. She asked her aunty where the convenience was and was told that it was at the bottom of the stairs, tucked under them in a tiny cupboard-sized place. As it was time for her to go she thanked her auntie for the tea and said her goodbyes.

She went to say goodbye to Lord but as he was still busy happily gnawing his bone she did not disturb him. She found Jake emptying the skip basket into the manure bin set on the cobbles outside, by the stable door. It was nearly full and would be emptied next morning by one of the vestry horse and carts that collected from all the mews stables every second day, probably to be emptied into a barge at their uncle's wharf.

She said goodbye to Jake, as she left the mews she walked past the back door of one of the square's grand houses and, on looking through the railings down into the basement kitchen she saw Jake's older sister preparing vegetables, they waved to each other. She was lucky in finding work close to home, and being able to see her family each day, unlike so many other girls who had to move far away and go into service in the houses of more fortunate people.

To Hilda, life in the yard seemed quiet without the antics of Lord and Quess. As she and Queenie got on with their usual egg hunt she gazed around and saw the butcher's boy trundling a freshly-painted wheel across the yard. A few days ago he had been swanking off, whistling at some girls and not looking where he was driving, he had badly skinned the wheel along the curb. He had just fetched it from the coach painter's workshop where it had been re-painted at his expense. The cart stood at an angle on one wheel, the other end of the Collinge axle resting on a stack of wooden boxes, waiting for him to lift the wheel on and do up the counter-threaded nuts that held it in place. The first one threaded clockwise and the second screwed counter clockwise firmly against the first. With a split pin through the hole at the end of the axle stub made it doubly secure, lastly the bright brass hub cap had a little oil poured in to act as a reservoir and was screwed into place.

Job done and he could resume his deliveries, this time taking a lot more care.

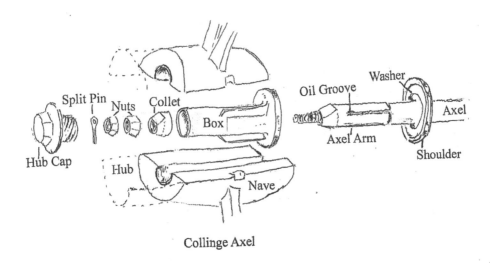

Collinge Axel

Chapter Four

It had taken some time but Hilda's father had made all the arrangements, which were rather complicated, Earl was to go to a titled family who live far away in the country. Though sad that he was going, she thought that this sounded a nice home for him as there were children there that he would be able to play with.

Towards the end of the following week mother gave Hilda two luggage labels filled in with the destination, one was to be tied to Earl's collar and the other one to be put on the wicker hamper that he was to travel in. Having had an extra nice breakfast with an egg and milk drink to go with his usual biscuits, his journey began. The cabbie who drove the old Brougham with its basket on the roof, and was now used as a Growler Cab, took Earl and Hilda to the station. Dropping them off at the entrance before going on to take up his position on the rank, ready to pick up a fare. They went through onto the concourse that was thronged with hurrying people, it was rather gloomy as the wide, arched glass roof which spanned it was grimy with smoke and smuts from the steam engines.

She found the right platform where a guard was supervising the loading of goods in the right order into the luggage van. A kindly little man who was on the lookout for her and Earl, he took one of Hilda's labels and tied it on to a big hamper that stood next to a pair of elegant gold-painted chairs stacked together and held with strips of hessian binding to protect their delicate legs.

The guard compared the labels. 'Ah' he said 'these are to go to the same destination'. He opened the basket lid, 'tie your label on to his collar and bring the little chap in'. Hilda hesitated, eyeing the rather wide and frightening gap between the van and the platform, the guard lifted Earl and placed him into the basket. 'Do you want to say goodbye to him?' She jumped the gap and bending down she kissed the black spot on the top of the little dog's head, it felt like warm silk velvet. 'Goodbye Earl, be good and lucky' she murmured as she produced a large piece of a hoof trimming from her coat pocket, She had saved it from the farrier the morning before. Earl took it in keen anticipation as the guard closed the lid and secured it with two straps.

Hilda jumped out onto the platform and the guard close the van's wide double doors. He then looked along the train seeing the last passengers slamming the carriage doors behind them, he gave a long shrill blow of his whistle and waved his green flag and leapt through a small door into his van. With a hiss of steam and loud chuffing puffs the engine lurched forward, and high-pitched clunking sounds came as the couplings of the carriages cach took up the strain, and Earl was on his way.

Earl lay uncomfortably crouched in the basket as it wasn't high enough to allow him to do anything else, but he had his curve of hoof to chew. Presently the ticky tock movement of the train lulled him into a light sleep, every now and then it stopped and sometimes the van doors were opened and some items of goods removed or taken on board before the whistle blew, and the journey started again. The guard shared his lunchtime snack, giving him the crusts off his sandwiches and the dregs of his strong sweet tea, drunk from the lid of his billycan. As Earl had been confined all day, the sacking on the floor of his prison had become wet and smelly, and he had sicked up some shards of hoof. He was feeling very sorry for himself when yet again the train came to a stop. This time the chairs and a few boxes were unloaded on to the platform and he could hear the guard talking to someone. Then the lid of his basket was raised, while he sat bemused blinking in the evening light, the lead was clipped to his collar, and a porter ushered him out onto a draughty platform where he was tied to a heavy barrow with the chairs on it. The train departed, taking his friendly guard with it, Earl felt lonely and lost.

He waited and waited and began to get cold. As dusk fell a very grumpy man came and loaded the chairs into an already full float, then yanking Earl's lead pushed him into a small space on its floor. All the while grumbling that he wouldn't have time to deliver the things they'd have to wait till the morning. Climbing into his seat and taking a swig from a bottle, he gathered up the reins and drove off. Though the Pickering Float was comfortably sprung by two side Leaf Springs it was a traumatic drive for poor Earl, he was glad when they pulled up in a yard, he received a kick as the man clumsy climbed out.

Putting the reins up on the cob's back, the man undid the breeching straps and chain-end traces. Feeling himself released, the cob walked forward and the shafts crashed to the ground, causing the floor of the float to slope so that Earl slid down, colliding painfully with a crate of bottles, and lay trapped under the chairs. The man stomped off following the horse into its stable and having unharnessed him, banged the door closed. Then he came and roughly pulled Earl out from under the seat. 'Come hear you smelly beggar' he said, as he dragged him into a derelict stable and slammed the door shut, leaving him alone in the dark. Next door he could hear the cob eating his supper, but there was no food or any comfort for him, he was tired, cold, hungry and thirsty, he had a little drink from a puddle below a patch of broken roof, through which he saw brightly-twinkling stars in the now frosty night air. He thought longingly of his mother and sister cuddled together in the warm stable at home, and of the supper that Hilda would have given them. He began to whimper and then presently howled and howled his unhappiness.

He heard a sound of footsteps hurrying over the cobbles and suddenly the door opened and there was a stout lady holding up a lantern that shone down on him. 'You poor little darlin' she said taking his trailing lead, 'Youm come along wie me', together they crossed the yard and went through a door into a scullery where it was warm.

She dipped a pail into the tub of the copper boiler, the water was still warm from the laundry she had been doing that morning, saying 'Youm are a smelly chap, we'll soon have you clean and nice again' as she washed him. He had to admit to himself that it was just what he needed after being shut in the horrid hamper all day. She poured water over him, wiping away the smelly stains 'til his coat was back to its usual immaculate state. He shook most of the water off himself, but she rubbed him dry with an old towel. Leaving him the kind lady went in to the adjoining room, pushing the door not quite shut behind her. Peering round it he saw the grumpy man sprawled snoring over the kitchen table amongst the remnants of his and the family's supper. The lady scraped the leftover rabbit pie and potato on to one plate, emptying the dregs of the gravy from the jug over them. 'Here you are' she said as she set the plate on the floor in front of Earl. Closing the door she left him in the dark, though it was not quite dark as the glowing embers under the copper threw a little light into the scullery, showing lines of clean washing hanging there to dry. Finding a basket of unwashed bedclothes on the floor he snuggled down in to their warmth and went to sleep.

Next morning Earl awoke with sunshine flooding into the scullery, he heard the sound of iron-shod hooves and wheels pulling up outside, a smiling young maid carrying a jug hurried through from the kitchen and out into the yard, leaving all the doors open. Curiously he followed and found her pink-faced shyly greeting a youth standing behind a milk float. The float looked similar to the one that he came in yesterday, though it was open at the back and had long sweeping mudguards. It was painted a cream colour with curly writing along its sides, a big brass churn stood on its floor. The top had been removed, and the youth dipped a long-handled can into it bringing it out brimming with milk that he poured into the jug. He was so intent looking in the maid's eyes he failed to noticed he was spilling some of it, Earl lapped up the puddle that had formed between the cobbles. 'We need butter and eggs' the maid said, with that the young man hung up the dipper on the top of the churn by its long

28

handle and opened the little louvered-sided cupboard that formed a seat, and took out a pat of butter wrapped in greaseproof paper. The maid gathered the lower corners of her apron and put the parcel into its fold, then reaching forward the lad took some eggs from the basket in the front and popped them in beside the butter. With that he gave the maid a kiss, mounted up and drove away at a smart pace. She stood for a while with a dreamy look on her face, as she turned to go back into the house one egg fell from her apron, smashing onto the yard. Earl quickly gobbled it up, shell and all. Now having had a satisfactory breakfast he accompanied her indoors.

The grumpy man seemed to be in a better temper that morning, he whistled tunefully as he harnessed up his cob and put him to the float. It still had the chairs and other goods in it, but he rearranged them, making room for Earl to ride comfortably beside him on a seat, though tied short to prevent him from jumping out.

In bright sunshine they set off into the early autumn countryside, the hedgerows beautiful with all kinds of berries, purple-blue sloes, dogwood and elder. A few late blackberries on their briars, with red and yellow leaves amongst the dark copper-green foliage, rose hips and hawthorn glowing brightly amongst them. The verges were neatly cropped short by rabbits who hopped away as they approached. Earl would have liked to chase them, but he was tied short to prevent him from jumping out. Now and then they stopped at a wayside cottage or farm, delivering some item from their load of goods or to pick up a new piece to add to their collection, they bowled along the dusty lanes at a steady trot until they came to a pair of ornate gates guarding a driveway. The gatekeeper was outside the lodge tending his garden that was filled with colour of chysanthemums, dahlias and michaelmas daisies, they exchanged pleasantries as the keeper opened the gates for them allowing them to pass up the avenue of lime trees.

Earl saw a of vista of grassland where a herd of deer grazed beneath the beech and elm trees, the leaves beginning to show their promised rust and gold colouring.

Beyond the sun-sparkled lake the land sloped upwards and there, shining pale in the afternoon sun, was an imposing house.

The winding driveway divided, the main part leading up to the porticoed front of the house but the float turned, taking the other path, passing through a shrubbery of rhododendron bushes and on through an archway topped with a clock tower into the courtyard. Earl had arrived at his new home.

The cob trotted round the courtyard as the clock softly chimed the third hour and Mister Grumpy pulled up at the back door. A stout important man took charge directing a footman to unload Earl's travelling companions, the chairs and take them indoors. At the same time a stable boy appeared as if from nowhere, he had been on the lookout eagerly anticipating the arrival of his new charge. He untied Earl and helped him down, taking him onto the square of grass in the centre of the yard, he patted him and read the name on the tatty remnants of the luggage label. 'Well hello Earl my name is Peter you come along with me' he said as Mister Grumpy drove away and vanished under the archway. Earl was not sorry to see him go as this new companion was much more to his liking.

Peter led him through a wide door set under the archway into a stable, here he felt quite at home in the familiar scent, sight and sound of horses standing in a long row of stalls as they contentedly pulled at their hay. Behind the door an extra big standing was used as a feed room, tidy with bins for oats, bran, beans and chaff, the sieves used while making the feeds up hung on the walls alongside the pitchforks, brooms and muck sheets and skip. Against the wall, lying on its side and wedged to prevent it rolling, lay a big barrel, still smelling sweetly of the cider that

it had once contained, but now it had had its end knocked out. In it a folded blanket lay over a quantity of fresh straw making a perfect draught-free bed. 'This is where you sleep my boy' said Peter as he encouraged Earl into it. Discarding the now rather small old collar that he had worn for most of his life a new one was buckled on, this had a brass rumbler bell stitched on to it, 'Now we will be able to hear where you are' Peter told him. Next to the barrel was a bowl of fresh water, Earl took a long drink before trying some of the pink, yellow and black oval biscuits that lay in a dish beside it, now he was ready to follow Peter and explore his new home.

He heard happy sounds of children playing and the sharp yapping of some small dogs, he went into the yard to see what it was all about and there were the children of the big house. They had come to meet him. They came through a side door from the garden throwing a ball for their Cavalier King Charles Spaniel and little Pug dog to run after. The dogs, on seeing Earl, went to him making the usual introductions on stiff legs with tails wagging, the children ran across the yard and joined in the greetings. It wasn't long until they were all playing chase with the ball under the watchful eye of the nursery maid who carried toddler Charles on her hip.

This was the first of many happy hours spent with the lively children as they all grew up together. He looked on as the young Lucy was taught to ride by her mother, like most girls, by altering the pommel of her saddle on alternate days she rode on either side of the saddle in order to avoid any enlargement of her hips or curvature of the spine. He was with her each day while she rode in the home paddock behind the coach house. Keeping well out of the pony's way as she learned to jump, her cries of fear soon changing to cries of delight as she became more proficient.

There were fine days when the Governess took the children for a breath of fresh air out in the Park, driving them in a small tub-shaped vehicle. With the door at the back there was no danger from the wheels to the children as they climbed in to take their seats facing each other, resting their backs against the high sides of the carriage.

The Governess drove from her sideways seat at the back beside the closed-door that had its handle set low down safely out of reach from naughty little hands. As Earl grew bigger and stronger he was able to accompany them as they trotted through the Parkland beside the safe, stuffy pony between the shafts. His name was Roary because his breathing made a roaring sound when he trotted fast. This vehicle was known as the Governess cart but when mother drove it was called the Nursery car.

The master of the house planned a visit to a friend who lived in the next county, he would drive himself there in his Mail Phaeton using the wheel pair of horses from his team of four. He expected to be away for three or four days and Davie, the under-coachman would go with him to look after the horses and act as his valet.

Even though the big doors of the coach house were wide open it was still rather dim inside but Davie had to get on with preparing the sturdy carriage for the journey. So he pulled it out on to the flagstones of the washdown under the glass roofed porch. Here he washed the Phaeton and dried it off with the chamois leather. Checking that the Telegraph springs and their shackles were in good order he squatted down to reach the straight perch that connected the rear axle to the front of the carriage, the running gear being much the same as a Mail Coach that it took its name from. Leaning over the splinter bar he smeard a little grease on to the turntable making a smooth easy turn of direction. Then he brushed the box cloth cushions and the lining of the hood before treating its leather and the dashboard and side mudguards with a waterproof dressing.

Interested, Earl looked on. With the help of the jack placed below the axle, each wheel in turn was lifted clear of the ground, the nuts of the long bolts undone and the

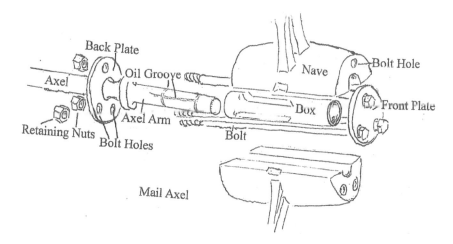

wheel removed and the axle arm oiled before the wheel was secured back on against the backplate and spun to check it ran straight and smoothly before being lowered to the ground again. To discourage any damp rusting the burnished bright shining polehead and chains they received a once-over with a oily rag, with new candles put into the lamps the job was complete.

The harness was ready as it had been put away clean from the last time it had been used. All that remained to be done for the journey was that the horses' shoes be checked. For this, riding one and leading the other Peter rode to the smithy in the village. Earl went with them trotting nearby as they passed along the avenue, the now-leafless branches still dripping from that morning's rain that had made the fallen crisp brown leaves into a soggy covering to the road. A sharp cold wind sent clouds scurrying overhead, both Peter and Earl were glad of the warmth from the fire of the forge as they waited while the horses were re-shoed.

The next morning with the pair put to the Phaeton, Davie drove it out under the archway and round to the front door. Earl went with them and stood by the carriage while the Master kissed goodbye to his Lady and the children. Then mounting up he took his comfortable seat on the Box and picked up his reins, nodded to Davie to step away from the horses' heads, and drove off while Davie was still climbing onto the rumble seat behind.

Peter only just managed to catch hold of Earl's collar to prevent him accompanying them, telling him that he was still too young to go all that long way and anyway he had seen a rat in the forage barn that morning that Earl must account for.

CHAPTER FIVE

Early in November the hunting season had started and the stable staff were run off their feet with work as Madam rode to hounds at least twice a week, often requiring a second horse.

Her favourite mount was an elegant homebred grey whose dapples diminished over the years as he grew older, but he jumped superbly. His name was Pegasus but as the small children found this hard to say he was known as Peggy.

On some days wearing her hunting habit she drove her Sporting Tandem to the meet. With one horse as wheeler between the shafts of the Tandem Cart while the leader, usually Peggy tip tupt gently along in the lead already wearing the side saddle and open bridle. On arriving at the meet her groom only had the breast collar with its long traces and the driving reins to remove and stow in to the carriage boot. Then Madam was ready to be legged up for her day's hunting.

On other days the head coachman drove her in the Waggonette to meet with her hunter that one of her grooms who was proficient at side saddle riding had hacked on to the venue.

Frequently Madam had friends who came to stay for a few days hunting. She had plenty of fit horses and was able to mount them. On these mornings the Waggonette was used. The carriage was conveniently entered from the back and six people could sit and converse face to face while leaning against the backrests.

As the season progressed and the weather deteriorated Earl was surprised to see that the Waggonette had mysteriously turned into a small Private Omnibus! This magic being wrought when the closed body of an Omnibus that he had previously seen suspended from the ceiling of the coach house, had been lowered onto the open back of the Waggonette and bolted into position. It then made a useful winter vehicle.

Earl accompanied this carriage when they fetched Albert and his trunk from the railway station on his return home from his boarding school for the Christmas holidays. The Governess had travelled inside to greet him and be companionable on the journey home, but young Albert would have none of that. In spite of the steady drizzle he took the reins and relegated Davey to the lower seat.

As Christmas time drew near and with shorter daylight hours combined with cold and wet weather the children did not come out to play as much as they had done before, they were cooped up indoors busy with their studies and the excitement of making decorations and gifts. Earl missed them a lot so was delighted when late afternoon on a misty day they all appeared and games resumed. Round and round the garden jumping the little hedges of the parterre and out on to the lawns, here the vista of the grazed Parkland merged with the short mown grass invisibly divided by a deep ditch and the Ha Ha wall.

George threw the ball, the dog scampered after it but their interest was taken by some fresh mole hills that had appeared just that afternoon and the ball rolled onwards and fell over the Ha Ha. 'Oh bother' said George as he stood looking at the ball now lying in the ditch, 'I'll climb down and get it' which he did even though the others told him not to. They watched as he negotiated the bricks jutting out of the wall forming steps. He had thrown the ball up to them and was almost at the top again when he slipped, falling into the deep ditch below. He lay there deathly white with his leg bent strangely beneath him, the other children ran shrieking into the house, it wasn't long before help arrived in the form of footman and garden staff, who gently lifted him and carried him to his bed.

The Master hurriedly wrote a note to the Doctor telling him what had happened and asking him to come quickly. He took it out to the stable yard himself and charged Davie to take Lionheart his best hunter and ride the eight miles into town just as fast as he could and put the note into the Doctor's hand. The big horse was swiftly tacked up and Davie was on his way, he did not bother with the winding little lanes he rode cross-country taking a direct route through the Park and farmland jumping everything that crossed his path.

Luckily the Doctor was at home, coming immediately to the door when Davie thumped on it. While the Doctor put together the extra things that he needed Davie went to his adjoining carriage house and quickly harnessed the hairy cob that he found there and had him between the shafts of the Gig so the Doctor could immediately drive it away through the heavy mist. It was a fast trotting cob and the Dennet Sprung Gig bounced and swayed as it sped along the muddy and rutted lanes. It had come on to rain and was nearly dark by the time the Doctor pulled up at the front steps. Peter who had been on the lookout ran forward to take the tired cob, assuring the Doctor that he would attend to him as if it were his own.

The cob was blowing hard, his sides heaving, his long coat wet through with sweat and rain. Peter led him round to the stable yard, stopping under the shelter of the archway, having released the breeching straps and traces he soon had the tired horse out of the vehicle and standing in the warmth of the stall that had been made ready for him, just as the Master had instructed. The cob, now stripped of his harness, Peter ran the scraper over him to remove the wet then ruffled his shaggy coat with a handful of soft hay before dropping a light wool blanket over his back, and checked his feet were free from stones. Having drunk his fill of the warm linseed gruel offered to him he tucked into a small feed of oats, bran and chaff, resting one hind leg he relaxed and made himself at home.

The Head Coachman himself had taken the two wheeler away setting it in the dry under the glass-roofed porch to make it ready for the Doctor's return journey. He wiped dry the well-stuffed deeply-buttoned leather seat cushions and back surround, put up the hood and cleaned the mud-splattered glass of the lamps with their bullseye glass that magnified the light from within. He opened the back of one lamp and pulled the little catch to release the stem, he unscrewed it and removed the half-burnt candle replacing

it with a fresh one. As he did so he admired the simplicity of how the candle compressed the spring within the stem, as the candle burnt it expanded to keep the lit wick up in the body of the lamp making it shine through the lens. Having attended to both the lamps he took the damp knee rug into the warm harness room and hung it front of the fire to dry.

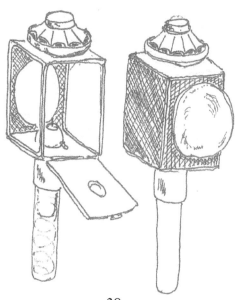

Davie had allowed Lionheart to stand for a little while in the cob's cosy stable before they started the long hack home through the lanes, following the same route that the Doctor had taken. Before long it came on to rain and turned pitch black, as he could see nothing he left it to the horse who instinctively knew his way home.

Peter, made sure that the cob's ears were now warm and dry before he left him and went about all the usual evening stable duties, attending to the other horses' comforts for the night. He put extra straw in Lionheart's loosebox, banking it up against the walls and making a deep bed for him.

In the harness room a pan of linseed simmered on the stove, he dipped out a mug full of the jelly and mixed it into a bucket of warm water making a restorative gruel for the tired horse.

Earl's friendly barking alerted everyone of the imminent return of the sodden pair. Davie left Lionheart to Peter to care for so that he could go to his quarters to get warm and into dry clothes.

There was a well-loved old lady who lived in one of the grace and favour cottages at the far end of the east drive. She was very special to the children, she had been their Nanny as she had been to their father and his father before!

For weeks they had been practising their carol singing and had lovingly been making gifts for her. They had been looking forward to Christmas Eve when, if it wasn't raining, they were all to walk down to her cottage to deliver their gifts and sing carols to her.

George was very cross, as he could not walk he would not be able to go with them, the others were just as disappointed. Their gloom was cheered by Mother suggesting that they used the Garden Chaise that Grandmother had enjoyed during her last Summer months. The little low Basket Carriage would accommodate George with his splinted stiff leg and its elliptic springs would make the ride smooth and comfy for him. Lilly the donkey, who worked in the garden and pulled the lawnmower in the Summer months was pressed into service.

It was a dry day, the afternoon though cold was overcast with heavy clouds that looked full of snow. They set off carrying the presents and special Christmas biscuits and shortbread that Evelin and Lucy had made themselves. Under the cooks tutelage they had spent all morning in the kitchen and were proud of the results. Earl went with them, he knew the way well as he often went there by himself. Nanny always seem to have plenty of biscuits that she generously shared with him and he looked forward to partaking of these new gifts.

It was a short visit, they gave her their gifts and sang the carols that they had practiced. They then had to hurry home because the clouds had started to send down their first flurries of big snowflakes. By the time they got home, much to the children's disappointment it had stopped snowing.

Earl was glad to be back home in the warm in time to supervise the evening stable routine and have his supper.

CHAPTER SIX

Earl loved his home, there was always something interesting to watch or to take part in. Mornings started early with the regular routine of keeping the stables fresh and clean, while the horses ate their feed the wet and soiled straw was tossed out of the stable and the floor swept. The muck carried away on a big sacking sheet to the heap where it was tidily stacked to rot down for the gardener's to use in the walled garden and hothouses where Earl was not allowed.

While the horses were groomed the head coachman went to the house to receive the carriage and horse requirements for the day. Which, When and Where as he called it, but seldom Why Whatever, the staff were always busy with carriages to wash and maintain, and horses to be exercised unless there was a particular job for them to do.

The outings with the Governess Car grew less as the children grew older, preferring the independence of riding their sprightly ponies or to drive for the sheer fun of it. Earl chose to accompany them going through the Park in all weathers and seasons. Often Madam would ride out taking young Lucy with her who proficiently rode her ponies that came and went, as she grew they progressed in height and spirit.

One afternoon the girls drove out together in the pretty Stick Back Gig to their friends' birthday tea-party. They were allowed to go alone as it was held at the house of the adjoining estate. Fortunately Earl had gone with them trotting beneath the axle, the three Dennett springs above him making a smooth ride for the girls in their party outfits. It was on their way home that what might have been a nasty incident took place. Two rough men waylaid them intent on some kind of mischief, the sisters

shrieked in terror but Earl ran forward in their defence barking at the men who quickly ran away. But, he could not resist the backside of the slower of the two men and gave it a good bite. He had never bitten anyone before and thought that he was in for a scolding when they got home, but he was treated like the hero he was and held in high esteem.

When Earl had first arrived Peter was just the young skip boy whose duties were throughout the day to pick up and take away the horses' droppings in his basket skip, so that the stables were always immaculate. He also had to keep the chaff bins filled with chop that he cut with the chopping machine. To do this hay was fed into its channel that had little cog wheels set in it, they tangled and drew the hay against the two sharp blades bolted to the wheel, as it turned they chopped the hay into inch long pieces, a backbreaking job for whoever turned the wheel.

This wasn't the only handle that Peter had to turn. In the Autumn and Winter months the clipping machine was kept busy removing the horses' long fluffy coats. These needed to be taken off so that the horses didn't get hot and sweaty when working and then stand shivering in a long wet coat. By the constant and rhythmic turning of the handle the sharp blades were rotated via a flexible metal cord and a clean smooth shave was achieved by a skilled groom.

Early in the New Year Earl noticed a pervading and unpleasant smell about the stables, this was made by the singeing lamp burning off the long cat hairs that grew in the horses' coats. While singeing these off to stop the flame from spoiling the fine coat beneath a quick swipe with a dandy brush was required. Perfectly safe and painless when done carefully

Earl enjoyed the friendship and chatter of the harness room where it was cool in Summer and cosy warm in the Winter. Over the years he watched as the harness and saddlery was cleaned and soaped to keep it soft and supple. How the bright steel bits, stirrups and pole chains were burnished before they were put away in a glass-fronted cabinet or placed in the wooden chest filled with drylime and bran, to deter the rust.

On Saturdays he went with Peter as far as the garden door to fetch the carrots that were then washed, dried and sliced long ways before they were placed in a little trug. Ready for Sir and Madam to give to their horses when they came to inspect them after church the next day. This was always quite a ceremony. The horses wearing their best colourful rugs were backed into their stalls and tied on the pillar reins to face out onto the passageway. The yellow Staffordshire floor bricks that were laid in a herringbone pattern shining pale and clean, from the scrubbing with a long handled broom that the stable man had given them the night before. Everything in its place cleaned and shining, even Earl's best collar with its gleaming bell.

The Winter had been mild, fill-dyke February was keeping up with its reputation. One hunting morning hounds were running fast on a good scent that had given an exciting long run. Madam and Peggy leapt over a hedge with a wide ditch below it, one that they had safely jumped many times before. On this occasion the far bank was so sodden and slippery the horse failed to find a firm foothold and fell, rolling back into the ditch.

They both died in the accident.

The following years life was a lot quieter, gone were the happy family outings and no guests came to stay arriving with their own carriages and horses. Then the stables had been busy, filled with strange horses and the staff slept in the dormitories above the stables.

In the coach house, The Park Drag coach stood forlornly under its dustsheet. Sir and Madam had loved to drive it with their matched team of bays in their Park while entertaining their guests, going on picnics and to the occasional race meetings where they had used it as their own private grandstand. Then the back boot of the coach was equipped with cellarettes filled with wine and food, with drawers for the cutlery and glasses. The Imperial box on the roof providing space for yet more food and picnicking requirements.

Young Peter had grown into a man and was so proud when he had been fitted with a livery coat and silk top hat, complete with a cockade that acknowledged his Master's position in life. White britches and top boots made him almost identical to Davie as they mounted in unison like mirror images to ride on the back seat of the Drag.

The children had also grown up, Charles was away at school most of the time, only returning home for the holidays and the older boys had disappeared. Lucy, always a free spirit, lived at home and continued to hunt and Evelin took over the running of the house for their father.

It seemed to Earl that the carriages were now pushed more closely together, crowded at one end of the coach house and strange new ones had been moved in. He was used to the double doors being opened and a carriage pushed out ready for the horses to be put to. Now instead nothing happened for a while, then with a great cough and bang accompanied by nasty smelling black smoke the carriage would appear, the coachman already seated and drive off by itself! Peter would often be with it but not in his bright-buttoned livery coat and cockaded top hat, of which he had been so proud. Now he wore dark breeches, gaiters and boots and a short matching jacket, topped by a severe flat top peaked cap that seemed so plain.

It was strange, the yard now housed fewer horses and life was a lot slower. Earl did not mind this too much as he was beginning to slow down himself.

Occasionally the boys would come home needing to be met at the station with the Waggonnette or the automobile. Some times they were brought by friends who drove an assortment of sporting carriages. Probably they came to see Evelin who had grown in to a lovely young woman and had quite a following, having the pick of beaus from a handful of suitable sons of well-to-do families. They visited her, seeking the approval of her father.

One of them borrowed his father's Curricle and drove it with great aplomb and swagger hoping to impress Evelin. She did not warm to this young fellow showing off in the fashionable Cee sprung two-wheeled vehicle. He explained to her how the pole between the horses was suspended from a bar carried on their backs and a strap went from under the horses' bellies over the pole. Thus preventing the whole thing from tipping down or backwards, and it was all beautifully balanced by his groom, who sat on the little rumble seat behind wearing his tiger-striped waistcoat. Of course Evelin could see how everything worked for herself, but just for something to say she enquired about the shiny elegant hook at the end of the pole. 'Oh, that is so that I can drive my 'four-in-hand', he proudly said. As he was not very competent with a pair she refused to drive out with him a few days later when he appeared with a team of four put to it.

He had to make do with younger sister Lucy who was always game for anything to do with horses. The young man showed off his supposed skill with his whip, waving it about unsettled the team, then when they saw the deer running over the open grassland of the Park they became too much of a handful for him to manage. Capable Lucy had to safely take them over, and that was the last seen of him, thankfully he never visited again.

Finally Evelin made her choice. Laurence was a banker and he wanted an ostentatious wedding in London, for the honeymoon he had procured passage for the maiden voyage of the Titanic, but Evelin would have none of it. She wanted a quiet wedding at home with a lunchtime reception. It was planned for early August so that the couple could go by train to his Uncle's estate in Yorkshire in time for the Glorious 12th and grouse shooting for a few days. Then continue up to Scotland to hopefully see the Northern lights. She chose the Victoria with its two seats as her wedding carriage and then after the reception it would take her and Lawrence to the station for their afternoon train.

The gardeners brought carnations and roses and masses of maidenhair fern to the coach house to decorate the vehicle. Making garlands to drape across the back from Cee spring to Cee spring and yet more to lie in the folds of the open hood. Davie and Peter as smart as usual had single carnations pinned to their chests, this as a token of the family's friendship to their servants on this special day, as normally servants never wore a buttonhole flower.

Earl, wearing a new collar for the occasion, watched the beautiful bride as her father helped her into the elegant carriage. He found it hard to remember how she had looked as a child when he had first met her as a ten-year-old girl on the day that he had arrived from London. He was so proud as he escorted her on her special day but sad when he saw the bride and groom depart into the railway station. Why he should be called the Groom when he obviously wasn't was beyond Earl's understanding.

It had been a happy busy day, the yard and drive unusually full of horses and carriages bringing those who had come on from the flower-filled church to the reception.

Now they had gone, and so had Evelin and her new husband and all was as it should be, but it seemed strangely quiet as he went to his barrel bed that evening. He remembered and thought of the days past and how happy and lucky he had been in his life. As he snoozed he dreamt of Dalmatian companions to their owners as they rode or drove their horses.

He heard the clock in the tower gently strike three times, just as it had when first he had arrived from London all those years ago, and he slept.

APPENDIX

Recently at a fashionable beach in South Africa I watched as a man sold ice cream from his tricycle vending machine. Amongst the gathered crowd of children was a Dalmatian and when the man moved further along the promenade the dog went too. Whether the dog was most attracted by the ice cream, the children or the fascination of the moving wheels I do not know. In these modern times the Dalmatian breed continues to be a popular pet who does its travelling in the family car. He or she may escort a pushchair or pram while walking out in the park, their inherent instincts to follow a wheel still running strong. A lucky few live in the country and horses are included in their lives and fewer still follow modern carriages that are too low for them to run under the axle in the traditional way as they go cross country and along quiet lanes.

The Author and her Friends wondered what might have happened to the characters portrayed in this book. Queenie probably had a litter or two herself and Hilda became a maid or cook somewhere and gone on to be a grandma.

Lord and Quess would have enjoyed their lives and died of old age happy in the service and friendship of their owners, likewise Earl who was buried under the square of grass in the centre of his yard.

Albert and Charles probably may have lost their lives valiantly but uselessly at the Somme or in the mud of Passchendaele alongside Peter and Davie.

George who had a pronounced limp would have gone into the church and been ordained a bishop. Evelin who had married well, went overseas with her husband in the diplomatic corps.

Whereas Lucy never married and during the war she may have joined the Army, working for Cecil Aldin the artist, who ran a remount depot and was the first to employ girls as grooms and roughriders. At the end of the war she returned home and continued to live on in the house where she bred children's ponies and hunted side saddle for many years.

The house was requisitioned in the Second World War and used for the rehabilitation of wounded airmen. On Lucy's death it was sold. For fifty years it became a girl's boarding school until by mismanagement it went bankrupt. Then the mansion and its capacious stable and yard were bought by a firm of developers who divided it into gracious apartments, for those who could afford them. Wanting a different and unusual name for the refurbished stable yard they, inexplicitly chose the name Earl's Yard.

Sometimes when residents returning home, after spending the evening at the gourmet pub in the village, see a small mirage of spotted light in the shadows. Maybe it is a wine-induced figment of their imagination, but they do feel a comforting and friendly presence.

Books written and illustrated by the same author

Donkey Driving
Make The Most Of Carriage Driving with Richard and Vivian Ellis
Tales Told To Greta
Recollections Of Joy